This igloo book belongs to:

....

igloobooks

Published in 2017
by Igloo Books Ltd
Cottage Farm
Sywell
NN6 0BJ
www.igloobooks.com

REX001 0317
2 4 6 8 10 9 7 5 3 1
ISBN 978-1-78670-590-7

Original story by Rudyard Kipling
Retold by Jenny Woods
Illustrated by Eva Morales

Cover designed by Lee Italiano
Interiors designed by Justine Ablett
Edited by Hannah Cather

Voiced by Blake Ritson and Katy Wix
Music and sound by Sam Park

Printed and manufactured in China

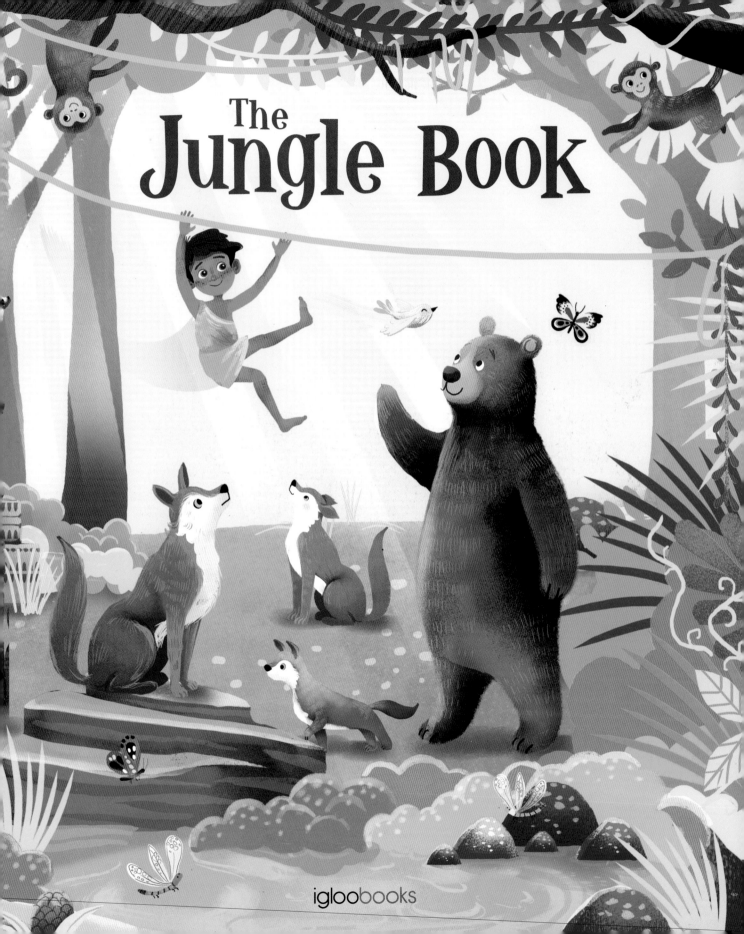

The Jungle Book

igloobooks

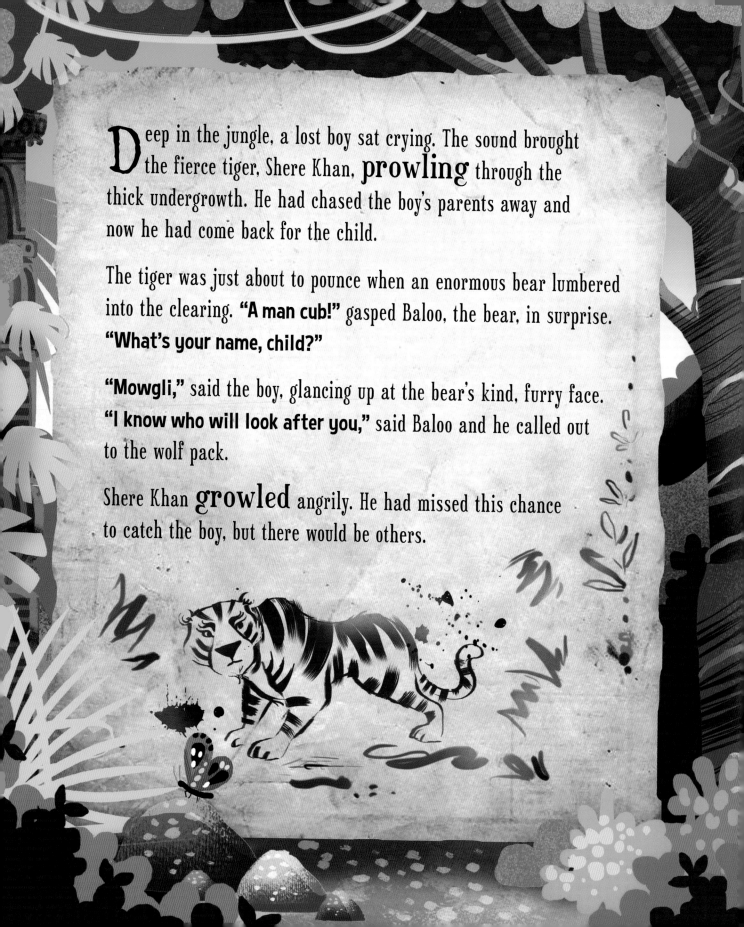

Deep in the jungle, a lost boy sat crying. The sound brought the fierce tiger, Shere Khan, **prowling** through the thick undergrowth. He had chased the boy's parents away and now he had come back for the child.

The tiger was just about to pounce when an enormous bear lumbered into the clearing. **"A man cub!"** gasped Baloo, the bear, in surprise. **"What's your name, child?"**

"Mowgli," said the boy, glancing up at the bear's kind, furry face. **"I know who will look after you,"** said Baloo and he called out to the wolf pack.

Shere Khan **growled** angrily. He had missed this chance to catch the boy, but there would be others.

Soon, Father Wolf and Mother Wolf appeared through the bushes.
"This is Mowgli," said Baloo, nudging the boy forward.

"Poor little cub," said Mother Wolf, giving Mowgli's face a gentle lick.
It tickled so much that he began to giggle.
"Don't worry, Baloo," said Father Wolf. **"We will take good care of him."**

Days later, Mowgli was playing happily with the wolf cubs. Suddenly, a furious **roar** thundered through the jungle and Shere Khan bounded out of the shadows. **"That's my man cub!"** he growled.

Mother Wolf leapt forward. **"Mowgli belongs to our pack now,"** she snapped. **"We will see,"** sneered the tiger, slinking away.

The next time the full moon glowed in the night sky, Father Wolf took Mowgli to the pack meeting.

Akela, the leader of the wolves, looked down from his high rock and asked, **"Why should we allow a man cub into our pack?"**
"Because Mowgli is my cub," answered Father Wolf, proudly.

Baloo held up a huge paw. **"I'll teach him the jungle laws,"** he promised. Then, Bagheera, the black panther, padded into the ring. **"And I'll watch over him,"** he purred. Akela nodded his head and all the wolves howled together.

Watching from his hiding place, Shere Khan **snarled** with rage.

So it was that Mowgli came to live among the wolves. Baloo taught him the ways of the jungle, and Mowgli would sit and listen to every **rustle** in the grass and every breath of the warm air.

But he would also hear the low **growl** of Shere Khan, as he **prowled** through the trees.

At night, Mowgli heard the **hoot** of owls and the **scratch** of bats roosting in the trees. Soon, even the **splashing** of the little fish in the pools meant more to Mowgli than anything he could remember from his life before the jungle. He was just like any other wolf in the pack.

When Mowgli got bigger and stronger,
Father Wolf taught him how to run and hunt.

Soon, he was as **fast** as any of the pack.

Bagheera showed him how to climb the tallest trees in the jungle. **"This is fun!"**
cried Mowgli, as he **leapt** from branch to branch, following the swift panther.

But Mowgli loved his lessons with Baloo best of all. The bear showed him where to find crunchy nuts and juicy berries...

... and how to ask the bees for their sweet honey.

When Mowgli got too sticky, he **splashed** in the jungle pools and Baloo taught him how to swim.

All the while,
Shere Khan watched...

... and waited.

As the years passed and Akela grew older and weaker, the tiger,
Shere Khan, came to be great friends with the younger wolves. He asked
them why they were happy to be led by an old wolf and a man cub.

Bagheera knew how dangerous Shere Khan was and warned Mowgli never to trust him. **"If you are ever in danger, fetch the red flower from the man village, for all animals fear it,"** he said.

The red flower was actually fire, but the animals were too scared to say its name.

After speaking with Bagheera, Mowgli went to find Baloo.
"I'm not scared of Shere Khan," he said, laughing. "I have the whole
pack to look after me, and in any case, I'm having
too much fun playing with the monkeys."

Baloo warned Mowgli that the monkeys were not
to be trusted either, but Mowgli wouldn't listen.

Then, one day, the monkeys **crept** through the trees...

... and **snatched** Mowgli while he was napping.

"Come back!" cried Baloo, but he was too slow.

The monkeys **chattered** noisily and carried Mowgli off to the ruins of the lost city. **"Man used to live here,"** said the monkeys. **"Now, it is ours."**

Meanwhile, Baloo found Bagheera sleeping on a branch.

"Wake up!" cried Baloo, tugging the panther's tail. "We need to save Mowgli from the monkeys."

Bagheera knew there was only one creature the monkeys were scared of. So, he asked Kaa, the snake, to help rescue the boy.

As Baloo and Bagheera entered the lost city, the monkeys **pounced** on them. Kaa lifted his scaly head and gave a loud ss**SSSS**. Shrieking with fear, the monkeys ran away.

"Thank you for rescuing me," said Mowgli, hugging his friends. "I'll never play with the monkeys again."

On the other side of the jungle, Shere Khan was plotting a way to get hold of the man cub. The cunning tiger had persuaded the young wolves that Mowgli did not belong with them.

"Akela is getting older and weaker," he said. **"It is Mowgli who will be leader of the pack when he dies."**

"But if you choose your own leader, you can give Mowgli to me," purred Shere Khan.

"It's true. The boy doesn't belong in the pack," said the young wolves. "He is not one of us."

Father Wolf was hunting nearby. He had heard everything and ran off to warn Mowgli.

Mowgli would not believe Father Wolf. **"Akela is still strong enough to lead the pack,"** he said.

So, Father Wolf took him to watch the hunt. They peered through the leaves as the young wolves called out to their leader, **"Why don't you catch that fine stag, Akela?"**

The old wolf gathered all his strength and **leapt** at the stag. It jumped out of the way and gave Akela a sharp kick.

The other wolves **howled** with laughter, but Mowgli felt sad.

"Akela can no longer protect me," he sighed. **"I know what I must do."**

Mowgli **dashed** through the jungle until he reached the man village. He crept up to one of the huts and peered through the window. Inside, a family were sitting around a fire, talking and laughing together. Every so often, one of them would get up and feed the fire with lumps of charcoal, which glowed in the flames.

Eventually, all of the family went to bed. Mowgli tiptoed inside the hut, quietly took a pot and then scooped some of the glowing coals inside.

Once the pot was full, he slipped out of the hut,
looking around to check that no one had woken up.

When he arrived, Mowgli was horrified to see Shere Khan sitting on the high rock, while Akela was slumped on the ground.

As Mowgli left the village, a howl **pierced** through the jungle.

"It is time for the pack meeting," he thought, clutching the pot of hot coals.

"Your leader is a toothless fool!" roared Shere Khan. "He is doomed to die!"

Mowgli sprang to his feet. "Does Shere Khan lead the pack? What has a tiger to do with our leadership?"

There were yells of "Silence, man cub! Let him speak."

"Give me the man cub," snarled the tiger.
"He is a man's child and from the
marrow of my bones, **I hate him!**"

The wolves yelled, **"A man! A man! What has a man**
to do with us? Let him go to his own place."

The young wolves gathered around, **growling** fiercely. Suddenly, Mowgli **jumped** onto the rocks, lifted the pot and threw its contents. The hot coals tumbled out, setting fire to the dry grass. Flames flared up around Shere Khan and he fled into the jungle, **yowling** in terror.

As Mowgli walked away from the fire, he knew it was time for him to leave his jungle home. He stopped when he saw his friends. **"It is not safe for me here any more,"** he said, sadly.

"You will be happy in the man village," said Mother Wolf and she licked Mowgli's face to make him laugh.

Mowgli turned to Baloo and Bagheera.
"Goodbye, my friends," he said.
"Thank you for taking care of me."

With a wave and a smile, Mowgli set off towards the village, knowing he would never forget his jungle friends.

Discover three more enchanting classic tales on audio CD...

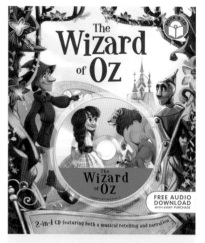

Join Alice and tumble down the rabbit hole into Wonderland, where nothing is as it seems. This beautiful book is perfect for creating the most magical of storytimes for every little reader.

Set sail on a rip-roaring adventure in this classic tale of swashbuckling pirates and hidden treasure. This exciting tale, with stunning original illustrations, is perfect for a thrilling storytime.

Be swept away with Dorothy and Toto to the Land of Oz, where they meet a talking Scarecrow, Tin Man and Lion. This retelling of the well-loved classic story is sure to make storytime exciting.

Scan the QR code below for your free audio book!

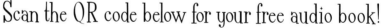

or visit https://igloobooks.com/bookandcd

igloobooks

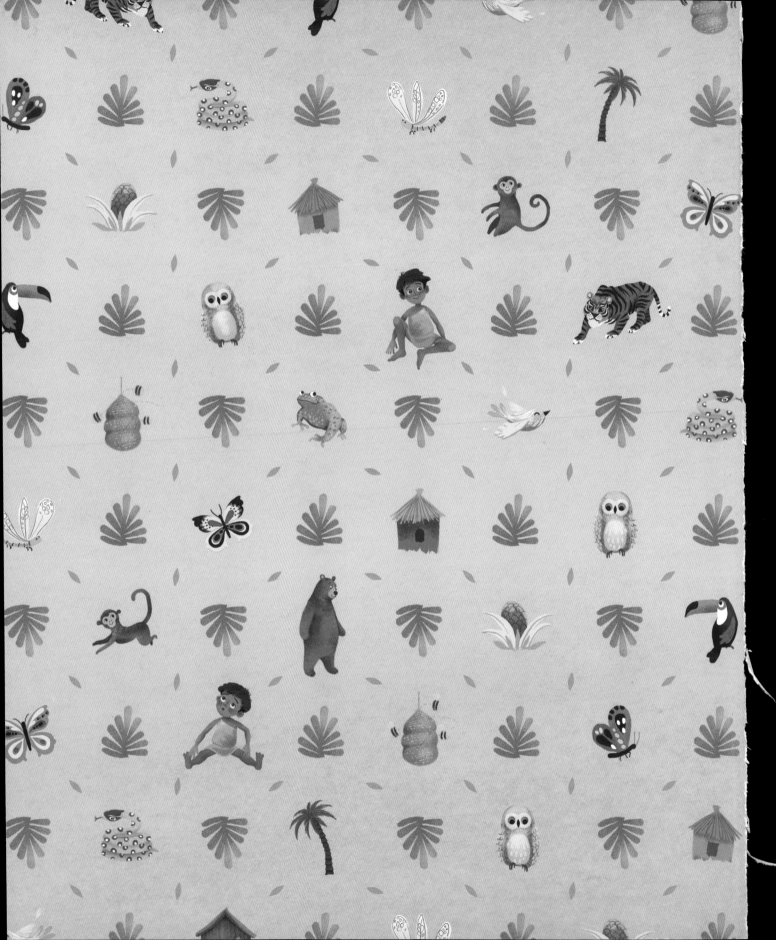